Where's Your Belly, Nelly?

by Wende Essrow
Illustrated by Bernice M. Smith

Recommended for children ages 4-8
and anyone who has a heart for dogs

ROCK - PAPER - [SAFETY] SCISSORS

RPSS - Rock, Paper, Safety Scissors Publishing, 429 Englewood Avenue, Kenmore, New York 14223
publisher@rockpapersafetyscissors.com • rpsspublishing.com

978-0-9977996-3-7 Where's Your Belly, Nelly? - Perfect Bound

10 9 8 7 6 5 4 3 2 1

Printed in the United States of America

To Harper Rose and her

great-grandmother, Amy Jane

Amy grew up around dogs —

lots and lots of dogs.

Her parents, Mr. and Mrs. Taylor, owned a school. It was not an ordinary school, it was a dog school and its name was, **No Naughty Puppies.**

People brought their puppies there to learn a few good manners and hopefully grow up to be great pets.

After school, Amy's bus dropped her off right at *No Naughty Puppies*, where her parents were running the puppy classes.

She had a little table behind the ring where she sat and watched the dogs.

She tried to get a little homework done, but the puppies were so cute Amy usually ended up bringing all her work home.

There were tall puppies like greyhounds, and Great Danes who wobbled on their long legs, and short chubby puppies like basset hounds, and pugs, who had trouble keeping up with the long-legged ones.

One time a pug got so tired he stopped and took a little nap on his way around the ring. All the pet owners thought that puppy was so cute.

Amy was six years old, but her birthday was coming soon.

Her parents promised her if she did her chores, like putting away her clothes, and if she did her best in school that when she turned seven she could pick out a puppy of her very own. For months she watched all the dogs in training to decide which type she liked best.

One day a couple brought in a sweet blond puppy named Nelly who Amy thought was the cutest puppy she'd ever seen. Nelly had big sparkly brown eyes, a tail as long as her body, and a soft golden coat.

The couple explained they were passing by and saw the **No Naughty Puppies** sign. Nelly's owners were moving into an apartment that did not allow pets.

Nelly was tired from the car ride, and sure enough she waddled over to Amy, plopped down on the floor, and rolled over.

Nelly showed off her sweet pink belly and fell fast asleep. Mr. and Mrs. Taylor saw the excited look on Amy's face.

Amy could not wait to get home from school the next day to see her very own puppy. As soon as she got in the door, Nelly wagged her tail so fast she knocked herself over. "Where's your belly, Nelly?" Amy asked, and then gave her puppy a tummy rub. Nelly loved tummy rubs! Nelly learned to roll over whenever Amy said, "WHERE'S YOUR BELLY, NELLY?" and get a tummy rub.

Amy was so proud she could not wait to show her friends Nelly's cutest trick. She taught her buddies to say, "Where's your belly Nelly?" and every time Nelly would plop down, roll, and get a tummy rub.

Nelly was very happy and grew bigger every week. She was finally ready for puppy school at **No Naughty Puppies**. Amy's mom let her go to the gift shop in the dog school and pick out a collar and leash for Nelly.

Amy loved purple, and she found a purple collar and matching leash that had tiny little black paw prints all over.

Amy laughed so hard at her silly pup she could hardly snap the collar in place.

It was finally the day to take Nelly to her first class at **No Naughty Puppies**. She knew Nelly would be the smartest puppy in school.

The first class was always about teaching the puppies the command, "Sit".

Her parents helped the owners show their puppies that if they said the word loudly and firmly then gently pushed on their dog's back end to help them sit, they would soon do it without any help at all.

Each time they heard the command and sat, they would get a little treat, and after a few tries they all understood

...except for one puppy.

Every time Amy said, "Sit!" in her loudest, most serious voice, Nelly would wag her tail, look at Amy, plop down at her feet, roll over, and show off her pink belly!

Oh no, thought Amy, *this is not working*. She asked her Dad to try. Even he could not make Nelly sit.

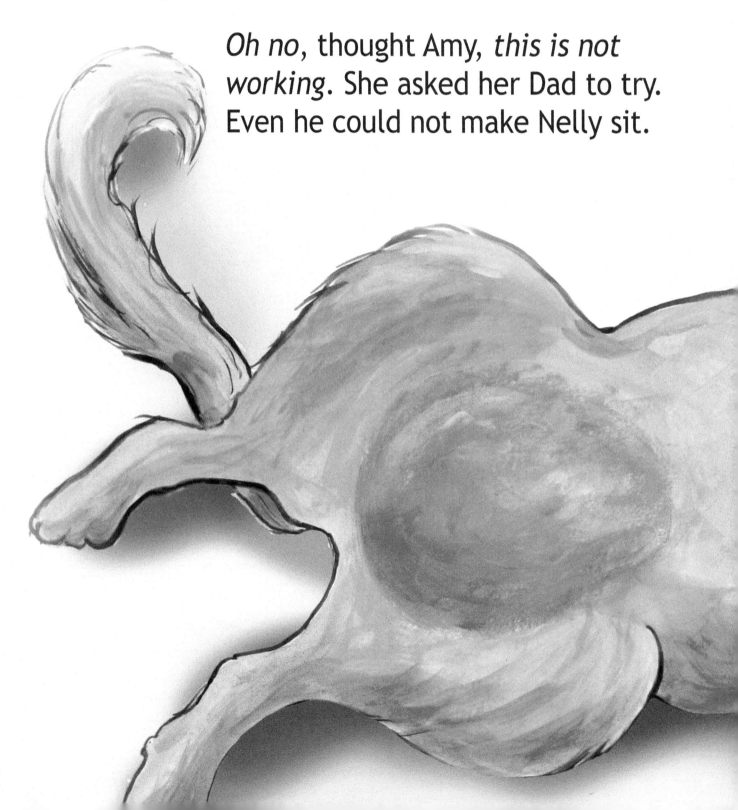

"She'll get it," he promised.

Amy practiced the "sit" command every morning before school, when she came home, and before bed too.

Nelly thought this was great fun because she got lots of extra biscuits but did not understand why. She missed hearing Amy say, "Where's your belly Nelly?" and would just show her belly anyway because that was her favorite thing —

that is, getting her belly rubbed.

The second week Mr. and Mrs. Taylor showed the owners how to say the command "Down," which meant lie down from a standing or sitting position.

Again, Amy tried and tried, and every time she said "DOWN," guess what Nelly did?

You are right. She plopped down, rolled over, and waited for a belly rub.

Poor Amy! How was her puppy ever going to get her blue ribbon at graduation, which was only two weeks away?

Mr. and Mrs. Taylor felt so bad for their daughter.

That night Mr. and Mrs. Taylor came up with a great idea for graduation and they kept it a secret from Amy.

Amy brushed Nelly's thick golden fur for an extra long time and begged her to try her best. They practiced "sit," "down," "stay," and "heeling," over and over. Nelly could do it sometimes, but usually Amy had to help by gently pushing her into position. Amy was worried all the other puppies would get their graduation ribbons except her Nelly.

"I will love you no matter what happens," she told Nelly and gave her a big hug.

Then the day of graduation arrived. All the owners were seated around the ring with their pets. There was Pointer, Max, T-bones, Ollie, Brewster and Nelly, of course. First they were asked to walk out in line and obey the command, "SIT". They all sat, except you-know-who. Nelly did her favorite trick: plop, roll, and show her belly.

Uh oh, thought Amy. *This is not going to go well. No prize for my girl*. Next, they all told their puppies, "DOWN," and sure enough, all the puppies had learned that command perfectly well other than Nelly, who was rolling around on the floor waiting for a belly rub.

Amy was getting really embarrassed. The next command was "HEEL," which meant walking nicely, right next to your owner's side, until you got around the whole ring.

Nelly started off perfectly well until she got halfway around and decided it was time for a belly rub — and down she went, almost tripping the owner behind her.

Poor Amy was trying not to cry.

Then she heard her father announce, "We have one more command that some of your dogs may know, and some may not, but it's very special."

Amy did not know what was going on, and then she heard both of her parents say into the microphone, "Where's your belly?" and right away Nelly was on the floor showing off her perfectly pink belly while all the other dogs were looking totally confused, and not one of them was lying down.

The whole audience and all the owners started to clap for Nelly, and Amy was prouder than anyone in the ring.

When her parents announced the graduation ribbons, Nelly was the first to be called. She won the hearts of the entire school, and was the sweetest little puppy in the whole world. After all, she had the rest of her life to learn how to sit, but she had already learned how to make everyone happy.

The End

CPSIA information can be obtained
at www.ICGtesting.com
Printed in the USA
BVOW05s2024210417
481649BV00002B/2/P